D1579802

SHADOW
SQUADRON

EAGLE
DOWN

2013.671

Raintree

SHADOW
SQUADRON

EAGLE DOWN

WRITTEN BY
CARL BOWEN

ILLUSTRATED BY
WILSON TORTOSA

COLOURED BY
BENNY FUENTES

2012.241

AUTHORIZING

RAINTREE IS AN IMPRINT OF
CAPSTONE GLOBAL LIBRARY LIMITED,
A COMPANY INCORPORATED IN ENGLAND AND WALES HAVING ITS
REGISTERED OFFICE AT 7 PILGRIM STREET, LONDON, EC4V 6LB
REGISTERED COMPANY NUMBER: 6695582

WWW.RAINTREEPUBLISHERS.CO.UK
MYORDERS@RAINTREEPUBLISHERS.CO.UK

FIRST PUBLISHED BY STONE ARCH BOOKS © 2013
FIRST PUBLISHED IN THE UNITED KINGDOM IN 2014
THE MORAL RIGHTS OF THE PROPRIETOR HAVE BEEN ASSERTED

DESIGNED BY BRANN GARVEY

ISBN 978 1 406 26655 9 (PAPERBACK)
17 16 15 14 13
10 9 8 7 6 5 4 3 2 1

PRINTED AND BOUND IN CHINA BY LEO PAPER PRODUCTS LTD

BRITISH LIBRARY CATALOGUING IN PUBLICATION DATA
A FULL CATALOGUE RECORD FOR THIS BOOK IS AVAILABLE FROM THE
BRITISH LIBRARY

CONTENTS

1316.991

SHADOW SQUADRON DOSSIER

CROSS, RYAN

RANK: Lieutenant Commander
BRANCH: Navy Seal
PSYCH PROFILE: Cross is the team leader of Shadow Squadron. He likes to be in control and insisted on hand-picking each member of his squad.

WALKER, ALONSO

RANK: Chief Petty Officer
BRANCH: Navy Seal
PSYCH PROFILE: Walker is Shadow Squadron's second-in-command. His combat experience, scepticism, and distrustful nature make him a good counter-balance to Cross's leadership.

YAMASHITA, KIMIYO

RANK: Lieutenant
BRANCH: Army Ranger
PSYCH PROFILE: The team's sniper is an expert marksman and a true stoic. It seems his emotions are as steady as his trigger finger.

BRIGHTON, EDGAR

RANK: Staff Sergeant
BRANCH: Air Force Combat Controller
PSYCH PROFILE: The team's technician and close-quarters-combat specialist is popular with his squadmates but often irritates his commanding officers.

LARSSEN, NEIL

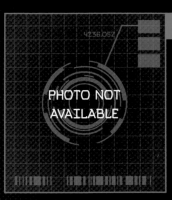

PHOTO NOT AVAILABLE

RANK: Second Lieutenant
BRANCH: Army Ranger
PSYCH PROFILE: Larssen prides himself on being a jack-of-all-trades. His versatility allows him to fill several roles for Shadow Squadron.

SHEPHERD, MARK

PHOTO NOT AVAILABLE

RANK: Lieutenant
BRANCH: Army (Green Beret)
PSYCH PROFILE: The heavy-weapons expert of the group, Shepherd's love of combat borders on unhealthy.

2019.681

MISSION BRIEFING

OPERATION

EAGLE DOWN 1234

This one's going to be a solo mission for Staff Sergeant Edgar Brighton. He will spearhead the joint-government effort to shut down the Colombian drug network, or nexus, that is mainlining illegal drugs onto US soil. The target is a shipyard along the Pacific coast in the Colombian jungle. Brighton will rendezvouz with local Colombian soldiers, assess the site, and call in an air strike to shut down the operation for good.

The rest of Shadow Squadron will assist Brighton remotely and await his signal for pick-up upon completion of the mission.

– Lieutenant Commander Ryan Cross

3245.98 ● ● ●

COLOMBIA

PRIMARY OBJECTIVE(S)

- Covert insertion via parachute

- Rendezvouz with Colombian task force

- Locate shipyard

- Call in co-ordinates for precision air strike

SECONDARY OBJECTIVE(S)

- Minimize casualties

- Foster positive relations with the Colombian task force

- Remain undetected

1932.789

0412.981

1624.054

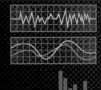

INTEL

DECRYPTING
||||||||| |||||||||||||

12345

COM CHATTER

- COMBAT CONTROLLER – an Air Force soldier who specializes in air support, communication, and organization
- TASK FORCE – a temporary grouping of units under one commander
- NEXUS – the core or centre, or the means of connection between several individual elements; an organization
- RECONNAISSANCE – a search made for useful military information in the field

3245.98 ● ● ●

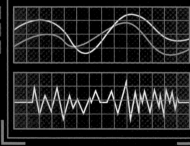

CHAPTER ONE

EAGLE HAS LANDED

Right up until the moment he touched ground in the jungle, Brighton's assessment of the mission was that *Operation: Nexus* was going just fine.

This mission was a joint US and Colombian venture aimed at striking a powerful blow to the illegal Colombian drug network, or nexus. Their primary target was a low-tech shipyard hidden somewhere in the roadless jungles along Colombia's Pacific coast.

Somewhere among looping rivers and mangrove trees was a facility that produced vessels capable of smuggling up to ten tonnes of cocaine at a time. And they were virtually undetectable.

These vehicles, nicknamed "narco-subs," were small fibreglass crafts capable of running just below the ocean's surface, guided by periscope and GPS. A small crew could take one of these boats from the shipyard, sneak down the riverways to the coast, and get to the ocean with ease. From there, the narco-subs headed north to the coast of Mexico. Then they docked in various concealed ports to offload their illegal drugs to waiting distributors.

In recent years, this system caused a sharp rise in cocaine coming from Colombia into Mexico then into the United States. The Mexican Sinaloa drug cartel cut, distributed, and sold the cocaine. Elements of the Fuerzas Armadas Revolucionarias de Colombia (or FARC) rebel guerilla army produced the cocaine. FARC also outfitted the narco-subs and recruited the terrified fishermen who piloted them.

When the Sinaloa cartel sold the cocaine abroad, it gave back a percentage of the profits to the FARC guerillas. The guerillas then used the money to buy weapons, equipment, and supplies for their ongoing attempts to overthrow the government of Colombia.

After a lot of talking about the problem and a lot of planning, the US and Colombia had decided on a strategy that would cripple the FARC/Sinaloa drug trafficking arrangement. The Colombians had some general information about where they believed the narco-sub shipyard was hidden. However, they had lost every soldier and police officer they'd sent into the jungle. Even worse, none of them were able to confirm the shipyard's suspected location.

The Colombians claimed they were committed to assaulting and shutting down the hidden shipyard. However, they needed help from the Americans to actually find the base and gather solid intel about it. They didn't want a large number of American troops and military machinery plunging into their backyard to fight their battles for them. Instead, they just wanted some help getting started.

That help came in the form of Staff Sergeant Edgar Brighton, a combat controller with the US Air Force. And, unknown to most, a charter member of the Shadow Squadron team.

Along with Brighton, Shadow Squadron was made of members from the Army Rangers, the Green Berets, Marine Force Recon, and the Navy SEALs. The Colombians welcomed Shadow Squadron to use the tiny military base on the otherwise uninhabited Malpelo Island. Then the Colombians set up a joint military and police task force of its own people to co-ordinate with the highly trained Americans.

They'd all been working and training together for a few weeks, and were now ready to put *Operation: Nexus* into motion. The first stage was to improve the Colombians' intelligence about the shipyard before an air raid kicked off the final stage.

Because of his unique set of skills, and fluency in Spanish, Staff Sergeant Brighton was chosen by Leiutenant Commander Cross for the role.

As a combat controller, Brighton's job was to head out alone into hostile territory and perform special reconnaissance. He would then report his findings back to Cross at their makeshift headquarters. In the field, it was his job to maintain contact with whatever aerial units were available. That meant Brighton had to organize fast-attack fighters, heavy bombers, and emergency air transport. He had to keep them on task, on target, and out of each other's way.

Brighton was also responsible for direct action. He stood side-by-side with his fellow soldiers when they engaged the enemy.

Plenty of air support was on hand for *Operation: Nexus*, so it was up to Brighton to get in first. It was up to him to make everything ready for the rest of his team. But he would not be alone.

To help him in this task, he was ordered to link up in the jungle with an advance team of Colombians from the military and police task force. They would point him in the right direction once he got his boots on the ground. Then they would watch his back while he gathered intelligence and reported back to Lieutenant Commander Cross and the rest of Shadow Squadron.

The ride by boat and then car from Malpelo Island to the forward staging base in Popayan had been pleasant enough. It gave Brighton a chance to shoot the breeze with his commanding officer, Lieutenant Commander Ryan Cross. He also got to chat with the Colombian soldiers who'd come to retrieve him.

Being members of an elite group of covert special operatives, Cross and Brighten couldn't say anything personal about themselves or their service records to the Colombians. But the local policemen and soldiers in the task force seemed to love small talk.

The pre-mission briefing between Brighton, Cross, and Major Timoleon Gaitan (the leader of the task force) had gone well. However, Brighton could tell the Colombian major was nervous about how young Brighton was.

Gaitan had kept his opinion to himself, though, so Brighton hadn't been forced to list the number of specialized training schools whose programmes he'd aced after Combat Control School. He knew he'd been selected for the Shadow Squadron at such a young age for very good reasons. But Major Gaitan didn't ask what those reasons were. That was probably for the best, though, as Brighton didn't want to embarrass his host.

The flight out over the jungle was just like the dozens of others Brighton had participated in all over the world. The passenger compartment of the Cessna 206 that the Colombian Police provided for transport was a little cramped. Or, at least it felt that way with the air crew, the jumpmaster, and Brighton's load of gear all jammed together.

Sadly, Brighton didn't have the time to chat with Popayan's team due to last-minute checks of his gear and parachute rigging. However, a few jokes and his pleasant manner seemed to set everyone at ease. That is, as at ease as men can be in a cramped, dark aeroplane cabin over hostile territory in the early morning hours.

But if anyone could pull it off, Brighton thought he was the man. He loved meeting new people and enjoyed nothing more than making new friends.

* * *

Just before dawn, the pilot said over the intercom that the plane was over the jump zone. Brighton donned his night-vision mask, then stepped up to the Cessna's side door beside the jumpmaster. With the mask's several 16mm intensifier tubes sticking out like fingers around his eyes, it gave Brighton an eerie, insect-like appearance. Brighton saw the jumpmaster do a double-take as he approached.

Strange looks aside, Brighton preferred the expanded field of view of his panoramic mask to the ones the rest of Shadow Squadron used. Those made him feel like his field of vision was limited.

Following the jumpmaster's pointed finger, Brighton located a tiny clearing a few hundred metres from the bank of the muddy river below. From its centre, a small infrared beacon blinked. That was the signal the Colombians' advance team had set up to guide Brighton to them. It was visible only via night-vision equipment from above, thankfully. Brighton didn't want to land amidst a team of armed hostiles.

Clearing his thoughts, Brighton readied himself to jump. From this height, it was going to be tricky hitting the bull's-eye on the clearing, but he wasn't worried. A pre-dawn precision jump into heavy jungle was nothing compared to having to deal with drug-dealing guerillas shooting at you. So, with a well-trained and fully confident mind, he awaited the jumpmaster's signal.

"GO!" the jumpmaster yelled. A moment later, Brighton hurled himself out of the door and into the darkness.

WOOOOOOOOOOSH!

The elation of his first few seconds of free-fall made Brighton's head swim. Skydiving had always thrilled him, ever since his first tandem jump with his father at the age of fifteen. He loved to let the thrill of the descent fill his mind as Earth soared up towards him.

But this time, he allowed himself only a few fleeting moments of joy before he let his training take over.

Brighton spread his arms and legs to right himself in the air and maximize wind resistance. Then he checked the altimeter and GPS device mounted on his wrist. Finally he shifted in the air until he located the target beacon with his goggles once more.

The easy, gradual turn gave him a good opportunity to observe the lay of the land. With his eyes, he traced the many river inlets and outlets, memorizing the few landmarks he could make out with his night-vision mask. When he was low enough, he opened his chute.

WOOOOOOSH!

Brighton bent himself into a wide downward spiral. He was confident that would put him within about ten metres of the clearing, if not dead centre. Easily, in fact.

The tricky part, however, was the actual landing. All of Brighton's gear made him heavy under the chute. As expected, Brighton managed to hole-in-one the small clearing. But when he hit the muddy ground, the extra weight made him stumble. A gust of wind pushed his chute into the branches overhead. Brighton was forced to leave it dangling for a moment to set down his secondary pack and squirm out of his rigging.

Standard procedure was to bury his jump gear after landing in order to minimize the chances that enemy forces would discover his intrusion. He had just opened his pack to grab his shovel when he heard several pairs of boots squelching through the mud.

Brighton saw a group of eight men in old-school camouflage uniforms emerge from the jungle shadows. They were ragged, hard-looking men. To

Brighton, they looked more like hardened special forces than policemen. And they all looked like they were quite a bit older than Brighton, though that could just be due to the wear and tear of years of combat experience.

"Hey, fellas," Brighton greeted them in Spanish. "Could you have picked a smaller clearing for my landing? I could almost see this one from the sky."

"You're the one Gaitan sent?" the one closest to Brighton asked. He had the gravelly voice of a lifetime smoker.

Brighton nodded. The man said nothing, but instead signalled to another soldier behind Brighton's back.

"Give me a sec to set up my radio," Brighton said. "If one of you could pull that chute down and bury it for me, I'd appreciate it."

Brighton knelt beside his pack. He'd just opened the waterproof flap and turned up the whip antenna when a man came up behind him. Without thinking, Brighton handed the folded-up shovel over his shoulder.

"Here you go," Brighton said. "I appreciate the help –"

ZIRRRRRRRRRRRRRT!

Fifty thousand volts of electricity poured into Brighton from between his shoulder blades. Every nerve and muscle in his body blazed with pain.

Brighton collapsed in a heap. He felt like he had no control over his own body. Brighton had endured this exact sensation before during his training. Otherwise, he wouldn't even know what had just happened.

In the back of his mind, far from the pain, Brighton understood he'd been zapped with a stun gun. No sooner had Brighton come to this realization when he received another jolt.

ZZZZZZRRRRRRRRRRRRRRT!

Brighton tried to yell, but his mouth wouldn't open. His teeth were clenched shut due to the muscles spasming through his entire body.

While Brighton lay gasping, one of the Colombians turned him over onto his back. The rest of the soldiers gathered around to look at him. One of them held the flashing IR beacon in his hand. At this close range, its intense glare stung Brighton's eyes through his night-vision mask.

A man knelt in front of him. He held the stun gun up where Brighton could see it. "He's still conscious," the man said. He lowered the stun gun at Brighton again.

It's not a knockout wand, man, Brighton wanted to say. But he was in too much pain to move, let alone speak. Fortunately, one of the other soldiers grabbed the stun gun out of the man's hand before he could zap Brighton again.

"Stop playing around," a voice said. Brighton glanced up to see the butt of an M16 assault rifle just as it came down hard on his night-vision mask.

KRUNCH!

Brighton saw stars and heard the sickening sound of shattering glass at once. Then he fell into total darkness.

* * *

When Brighton finally regained consciousness, he had no idea how long he'd been out. It could have been hours, or even days.

It probably wasn't days, but Brighton had no way of knowing. The only thing he knew for sure was that his head felt like it had been split wide open. A heavy, blinding throb emanating from above his right eye pounded in time with his pulse. *That would be where the Colombian smashed me in the face with the butt of that M16,* he realized.

As his senses returned, he scanned the area to take stock of his situation. Turning his head gingerly on his stiff neck, he saw that he was inside a large room on top of a concrete slab. It had a corrugated metal roof and walls.

The air was filled with jungle humidity, and the room lacked any sort of ventilation. What the room did have was bright lights on the ceiling and on the wall in front of him. They shone right in his face. Brighton could also hear a generator rumbling behind one of the walls.

Brighton tried to raise a hand to shield his aching eyes from the glare. But when his hand didn't move, he realized his wrists had been handcuffed to the chair he was sitting in.

The old dentist chair was upholstered in cracked, faded vinyl. As he glanced down at his ankles, he noticed they were cuffed to the footrest sticking out in front of him. His boots and socks were gone.

"FARC," Brighton grumbled.

There was no question he'd been captured by the very same FARC rebels that Shadow Squadron and the Colombian government were working together to bring down.

The only real question was what the guerillas who'd captured him had done to the real joint military/police task force. They were supposed to meet Brighton at the drop point. The fact that the FARC guerillas had been waiting around the IR beacon for Brighton implied that much. And the fact that they'd mentioned Major Gaitan by name proved that Brighton's capture hadn't been a result of dumb bad luck.

Brighton concluded that someone on the advance team was a traitor. That person could easily have warned the rebels about *Operation: Nexus*. But the sinister feel of the room in which Brighton found himself suggested that FARC had probably used torture to extract the information.

And Brighton fully expected that he would be next.

IIII∎III II∎III∎IIII∎III 5514.108

INTEL

DECRYPTING
IIIII∎III II∎III∎IIII∎IIII

12345

COM CHATTER

- CARBOY – a large container used to store various liquids, including water

- DRUG CARTEL – a criminal organization focused on drug trafficking

- FATIGUES – a soldier's uniform

- WATERBOARDING – form of torture in which water is poured over a person's face, causing the individual to feel like they are drowning

3245.98 ● ● ●

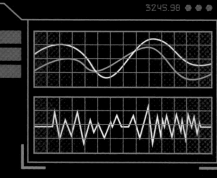

CLIPPED

CLINK!

Brighton heard a door open behind him. A Colombian man slowly walked around him into view. He wore clean olive-drab fatigues, rubber gloves, and a baby-blue surgical mask. Only his eyes were visible beneath the brim of his hat. He was writing a note in a small, spiral-bound notepad when he noticed that Brighton was awake.

The man tucked his pad and a pen into his hip pocket and checked Brighton's pulse. Then he prodded gingerly at the lump over Brighton's right eye. Brighton eyed him warily through his examination. The man said nothing.

"Can I have some water?" Brighton asked.

The Colombian still said nothing. "Maybe a sandwich? I'd name some names for a Philly cheese steak right about now."

The Colombian stood up, then walked behind Brighton to the entrance.

"And bring me some aspirin when you come back," Brighton called out. "My head is killing me."

The door opened, then quickly closed behind him. "All right, take your time," Brighton said. "Think about it."

Another ten minutes or so went by. Then the door opened and several sets of feet shuffled inside. Nobody came around into Brighton's field of view at first, but he heard them moving around behind him. Someone kept making trips in and out. The person's breathing was strained by carrying something heavy. It took a couple of repetitions before Brighton realised what it was. Someone was carrying in heavy plastic carboys full of water, like the ones that plugged into the top of office water coolers. By Brighton's count, they brought in a total of six containers.

When that was done, someone dragged in a rolling cart then shut the door. Only then did the visitors finally come into Brighton's line of sight.

On his right came the same Colombian whom Brighton had seen before. Now the gloves and mask were gone, but the pen and pad were still in his pocket. He wore a stethoscope around his neck, and held an ophthalmoscope in his hand.

The man leant over Brighton and used the opthalmoscope to peer into his eyes. Then he checked Brighton's heartbeat and breathing with the stethoscope. Not once did the man's eyes meet Brighton's.

Behind the "doctor" stood two more Colombians wearing camo fatigues. Brighton recognized them from the clearing in the jungle. One of them was the guy who'd zapped him with the stun gun. The other was the one who'd knocked him out with the rifle.

"Hey, man," Brighton said to the man examining

him. "Where's my aspirin?"

Someone else came up on Brighton's left. "Good morning," a low, quiet voice said.

Brighton was quite surprised by the voice. For one thing, the speaker used English with a Spanish accent. Brighton wasn't all that great with languages, but he was pretty sure the speaker was Mexican, not Colombian. That almost certainly meant she was on loan to the FARC guerillas from the Sinaloa drug cartel in Mexico.

More good news, Brighton thought sarcastically. *That means she's a hired professional.*

Yet Brighton was more surprised that the speaker was a woman. As she stepped into view, Brighton saw she was wearing a loose cotton blouse buttoned up over a black tank top. Her dark green fatigues were tucked into camouflage combat boots. She appeared to be in her mid-thirties, and in excellent physical shape.

"My name is Morgan Saenz. I represent the Sinaloa cartel," the woman said.

Brighton grimaced. *I hate being right all the time,* he thought.

The woman pushed a steel tray on a rolling metal cart up to the side of Brighton's chair, then stood next to it. A white hotel-style hand towel covered a handful of mysterious lumps on the tray. Her fingers danced over the lumps while she looked Brighton right in the eyes.

"It doesn't concern me that you know my name, young man," Saenz said. "Let that explain to you the situation you are in. It doesn't matter how much information you learn about me or our operation here. That is because you'll never have an opportunity to reveal it to anyone."

"Why's that?" Brighton asked, despite knowing the answer perfectly well.

"Because we're going to kill you," Saenz said flatly. "Only the circumstances of your death are up to you. If you answer my questions freely and in detail, I'll see to it that you drift off to peaceful sleep and never wake up. If you resist me at first but eventually break down and co-operate, I'll reward you with a large-calibre bullet through the head. An equally quick death, if not so peaceful."

Saenz paused a moment for effect and stood in front of Brighton's chair. The harsh lights on the wall behind her cast her face in shadow. It made a halo of light shine through her long, black, shining hair. Brighton had to admit that it was an intimidating sight.

Yep, Brighton decided. *She's definitely not new to this.*

"But listen carefully, though, to what will happen if you test my patience," Saenz told him. She leant over and gripped the arms of Brighton's chair. She put her face right in front of his. "I fully expect you to resist at first. I wouldn't respect you if you didn't. But if you keep it up too long, I will punish you. If you still refuse to co-operate, your punishment will get worse. Eventually, there will come a point when I'm no longer interested in your co-operation."

Saenz stood back, then paused. She placed her hands on her hips, and said, "When that happens, I'm going to see to it that you die in more pain than you can possibly imagine. Nothing you say or do can save you at that point. Even if you try to co-operate, I won't change my mind. Do you understand?"

"You're making yourself pretty clear," Brighton said quietly.

"Good," Saenz said. She stood. "Now, this will be your best opportunity to start talking. Do you have anything to say?"

"Yeah, actually," Brighton replied. "For an older lady, you're pretty hot."

Saenz shook her head in disappointment. "Oh well," she said with a sigh. "It was your opportunity to waste."

Brighton gave his best attempt at a shrug. "I got to be me," he said with a grin.

Saenz looked over to the doctor and the two FARC guerillas behind Brighton. At a nod from her, the doctor pulled down the back of Brighton's chair.

THUD!

Brighton lay on his back staring up at the harsh lights on the ceiling. He struggled against his restraints and tried to pull himself back upright, but he couldn't move. He could only watch helplessly as the camouflage-clad guerillas shifted behind him.

Saenz lifted the hand towel from her tray and handed it to the doctor, who came around to the top of Brighton's chair. The doctor wrapped the towel around Brighton's face. He fastened the towel in place and stepped back. The guerillas moved forward.

When Brighton heard the sound of sloshing water, he realized what was about to happen. He took a deep breath. A second later, the guerillas popped the valve in the top of the plastic carboy they carried between them and upended the whole jug over Brighton's head.

SPLASSSSSSSSSH!

The water was shockingly cold. It immediately soaked the towel over Brighton's face, turning it into an icy hand clamping down over his mouth and nose.

SPLASH! SPLASSSSSSSH!

The water came down and down and down, threatening to go on longer than Brighton could hold his breath. It ran up his nose and would have made him panic if he hadn't been expecting it.

Fortunately, the water in the carboy ran out before he had to breathe again. His lungs burned, but he made it through the first torrent without freaking out and filling his lungs with water.

"Are you new at this, or something?" he asked, spitting out water and trying not to gasp too loudly. "You're supposed to ask me some questions *before* you waterboard me."

"That was just a demonstration," Saenz said as she picked something up off the metal tray beside the chair. "I want you to understand that we're not opposed to hurting you."

"I'll remember that if you ever do hurt me," Brighton joked.

That comment got a chuckle out of Saenz, which Brighton considered a small victory.

"Our purpose is to gather information," Saenz said. "The soldier we brought here before you – the one you were supposed to meet, in fact – was not very helpful to us before he died."

"I wondered how you guys got the drop on me so fast," Brighton said. Behind him, he heard the guerillas picking up and opening another water carboy. Still flat on his back, Brighton listened for sound cues that they were about to dump it on him so that he'd know when to hold his breath.

"You know I'm not going to talk, though, right?" Brighton said.

"Not at first," Saenz said. "But do remember what I said about resistance. A stubborn waste of my time will be punished severely. So, let's start simply with some control questions. What is your name, what branch of the American military do you represent, and what is your rank?"

Brighton took a moment to collect his thoughts and prepare himself for what was coming. In his torture-resistance training, his instructor had taught him to think of something he loved that made him

happy. By holding onto that thought, the pain was easier to manage. For Brighton, that thought was the superhero comic books he read every chance he got.

Brighton grinned. "My name is Bruce Banner," he said. "And you're starting to make me angry. You wouldn't like me when I'm angry."

Saenz frowned. She gestured to the men behind Brighton. Instantly, several litres of water came down on him. Thankfully he heard the carboy slosh, so he was able to get a small breath in before any water hit him. He expected it to go on like it had before, but it stopped suddenly and the guerillas backed off.

Brighton expected the question to be repeated, but Saenz had another idea. She hit the trigger on a stun gun and let the electricity sizzle for a second so Brighton could identify the sound. He didn't even have time to struggle before Saenz turned the crackling weapon on him, touching his left thigh just above the knee.

ZZZZZZZZZZZIRT!

She only did it for a second, but it was more than enough. The second she stopped, the guerillas poured out water again.

SPLASSSSSSSSSSSH!

This time, Brighton had no way to hold his breath. Wracked with pain by the stun gun, his body instinctively tried to breathe. He sucked in water instead. His body immediately switched to panic mode. His mind began to scream that he was drowning, drowning, drowning!

It was all Brighton could do to force himself not to breathe in or out. He just locked his chest muscles and willed himself not to cough, not to gag, not to cry out. He forced himself just to hold on and ride out the pain as best he could.

Fortunately the second rush of water stopped as quickly as the first one had. He held his breath for another couple of seconds just to be sure, then sucked in an icy, wet lungful of water that made him cough and choke.

"Perhaps you misunderstood the question," Saenz said. Brighton's heart was beating so loudly in his ears that he could barely hear her. "What is your name, what branch of the military do you represent, and what is your rank?"

Brighton recalled his second favourite comic book. He coughed. "Okay, okay, I'll tell you!" he said, sounding as serious as possible. "I do work for the United States government. In fact, I'm part of a secret team called The Avengers. My real name is Steve Rogers . . ." Brighton stopped for a moment to catch his breath. ". . . But the world knows me as Captain America."

ZIRRRRRRRRRT!

Another jolt of electricity hit Brighton, cutting him off. It was longer this time. Then more water.

Brighton fought his panic instincts as best he could, but his head had tilted back from the shock, and the water hit him right in the nose. For a while, his entire world was like being trapped under the ocean waves. He coughed so hard that white lightning bolts criss-crossed behind his closed eyelids.

Then, somehow, it was over and he could breathe again – barely.

"Your name, your branch, your rank," Saenz said matter-of-factly. "These aren't even the difficult questions."

"My name . . ." Brighton croaked, ". . . is Batman."

* * *

After the first few rounds of questioning, Brighton lost the ability to mark the passing of time. It seemed to go on for hours. Half a day, at least. Maybe longer. The constancy of the lighting and the minimal variation in temperature blurred everything into a meaningless haze as his tormentor worked him over.

Throughout the ordeal, Brighton convinced himself that he was winning a small victory through sheer stubbornness. A session like this, he knew, was all about the balance of power between torturer and victim, and he was determined to hold on to whatever scrap of power he could. If he was able to resist giving information to the enemy, great. But if he could actively annoy the enemy in the process, he was at least playing the game by his own rules.

The Air Force's SERE (Survival, Escape, Resistance, Evasion) training after Combat Control School had helped prepare Brighton somewhat for this kind of situation. Part of the training dealt with how to steel yourself against the rigours of torture, such as holding on to your favourite memories.

But there were no secret techniques to magically make someone immune to pain, fear, or exhaustion. No, the largest part of resistance training had been more about describing common forms of torture and demonstrating what sensations those techniques inflicted on the human body.

Removing the element of the unknown from the equation made the idea of torture less intimidating. The instructors could then work with students one-on-one to try to help them find the individual emotional strength within that would help them survive against the enemy in the darkest of times.

That said, there was a marked difference between being taught what to expect from an "enhanced interrogation" and actually being subjected to torture. One of the lessons Brighton remembered most clearly from his very first day of SERE training was his grizzled, leathery instructor telling the class that torture breaks everyone eventually. There was only so much the body could take before the mind collapsed. Even Captain America would eventually turn into a willing collaborator.

No, the best a captured soldier could do was to keep his eyes and ears open for the means to escape when it presented itself. Brighton had already taken a step towards that goal, but the means were worthless without the opportunity.

That meant that he had to endure whatever Saenz and her lackeys dished out until they got frustrated enough to leave him alone for a while.

So, Brighton dug deep and refused to give in to the fear and desperation that welled up whenever Saenz's stun gun jolted him and the water came rushing down. He let himself cough and choke and hack, but he just kept telling himself that no matter how bad it got, it was too early for Saenz to really, truly want him dead. As far as she knew, he had information she valued. He didn't believe she was ready to let him die, so he had no fear – well, a diminished fear – of what she would do to him.

At some point during that first session, Saenz slowed down. Brighton could tell that his stubborn behaviour was getting to her. After the fifteenth time asking him the same question about who he was, then getting superhero names in response, she changed tactics.

Now she asked broader questions. How many Americans were working with the Colombians on *Operation: Nexus?* How long had they been ordered to stay in Colombia? What did they know about the specifics of the Sinaloa-FARC smuggling operation? Who was Brighton's commanding officer?

Saenz gave Brighton a long pause after asking each question, then signalled to her goons when he disappointed her.

During that phase of the interrogation, she gave Brighton a basic outline of the areas of concern the leadership of the Sinaloa-FARC operation had about the American presence. It felt like a minor victory to Brighton – that he was getting far more information from his own torturer than she was able to get from him.

Finally, as that phase neared its conclusion – and the water in the carboys ran low – Brighton realized he was weakening. He didn't feel any nearer to collaborating than he had been before, but his body was worn out from all the abuse.

He let three questions go by without being able to come up with a comics reference in place of an honest answer. It had come to the point where Saenz was punishing him for silence rather than wilful disobedience. At last, the tone of her voice suggested that she realized they'd hit a wall.

"I suppose you'll be glad to know that's all for now," Saenz said.

The doctor in olive drab peeled back the sodden hand towel from Brighton's face and leant over him to check his vitals again.

"I probably should have given you a break some time ago," Saenz said, "but I was impressed by your extensive comic book knowledge. You and I, it seems, have surprisingly similar tastes in reading."

"Cool," Brighton tried to say, through his throat was too raw to speak very loudly. "So you wanna go get a bite to eat together?"

"I'll pass," Saenz said. "Another reason we stayed so long today was that I wanted to convince myself whether this method of questioning was likely to have any effect on you in the long term. You might be proud to hear that it doesn't seem very effective. Therefore, when next we meet, I'll be upgrading the punishments you earn."

"Maybe next time you could try some positive reinforcement," Brighton said, his voice mockingly helpful. "Maybe bring me an ice cream cake or nice rib-eye steak. You know, I haven't seen the new Batman movie yet . . ."

"I have something else in mind," Saenz said. "Allow me to demonstrate."

She picked up something from the steel tray beside Brighton and flicked her wrist like she was cracking a whip.

SHINK!

Brighton recognized the distinctive sound the object made. Saenz had just whipped open a collapsible baton.

"That don't sound like ice cream cake," Brighton said.

Saenz said nothing. With a cold, grim expression, she walked past the end of the chair and raised the baton for a backhand swing. Brighton began to say something to change her mind, but she quickly struck him across the soles of both bare feet.

THWACK!

THWACK!

THWACK!

Saenz didn't put much power into the blow, but that didn't matter. Brighton howled as pain exploded up his legs.

SHINK!

Saenz collapsed the baton. Carefully, she placed it back on the tray. Brighton did his best to remain silent, but he couldn't stop his body from shaking due to the pain.

"Something for you to think about while I'm gone," Saenz said. Her voice was thick with self-satisfaction at Brighton's obvious suffering. "That's how I'll be punishing you for unhelpful answers during our next session. From now on, every session you force me to put you through will be worse than the one before."

She leant back over Brighton, then pulled the back of his chair upright so that he was sitting up again. Her voice dropped to a secret whisper.

"Thus far, I'm neither bored nor impressed with you, young man," Saenz said. "Most soldiers your age can make it through at least two sessions with me with their dignity still intact. Any more than that, though . . . and you'll get to see what I look like when I am angry. And believe me, you wouldn't like me when I am angry."

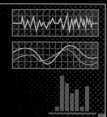

INTEL

DECRYPTING
||||| ||| ||| ||| ||| ||| |

12345

COM CHATTER

- AIR STRIKE - bombing attack carried out by an aircraft

- BRASS KNUCKLES - any type of metal attached to the fingers to increase damage done by punches

- M16 - assault rifle also known as the AR-15 that is capable of full-auto fire

- SLEEP DEPRIVATION - a form of psychological torture inflicted by keeping the victim awake for an extended period of time

3245.98 ● ● ●

WINGS

Alone now, Brighton's beaten-down body could have done with some quality rest. Unfortunately, sleep was out of the question.

For one thing, it was too hot to sleep. The blazing sun over the humid South American jungle turned the metal-and-concrete room into a stifling oven. Also, the lights glared down on him from every angle, which would've been far from restful even in peaceful circumstances. He might as well have been staring at the sun.

Of course, that was the point. Bright lights and uncomfortable temperatures kept a man from sleeping, and sleep deprivation contributed to the collapse of a man's judgement and willpower.

That was torture in and of itself.

Brighton couldn't allow himself to sleep now, anyway. He had no idea how long it would be before Saenz and her goons came back. The last thing he wanted was to let them catch him in the act of what he was about to do. He imagined they'd only be rougher on him if they discovered he was trying to escape.

Brighton had stolen the means of his escape the moment Saenz had introduced herself. When the FARC guerilla doctor had leant over Brighton with the ophthalmoscope to look in his eyes, Brighton slipped the retractable ballpoint pen out of the man's hip pocket. He then pushed it down into the padding on the arm of his chair through a crack in the ancient vinyl that covered it.

During his interrogation, Brighton had kept his forearm over the rip and the bulge the pen made. No matter how much it hurt, he hadn't moved. Otherwise, his captors would have spotted it.

Now that he was alone, Brighton worked the pen back out of its hiding place. To Brighton's red and weary eyes, the cheap piece of plastic junk looked like a treasure made of gold for one simple reason: it had a flat, detachable metal clip.

Carefully, to ensure he didn't drop the pen, Brighton slid his fingernail underneath the clip and bent it back until it stood out from the body of the pen at a right angle. Then he turned the pen upside down in his hand. Barely breathing, he inserted the end of the clip into the keyhole of the handcuff holding his right hand.

When it was firmly in place, he used the pen for leverage and bent the end of the clip into a right angle.

Brighton pulled the clip out and turned the pen around in his hand. Then he reinserted the bent clip and bent another right angle into it going the opposite way.

Despite the urgency of what he was doing, Brighton worked slowly and steadily as if he had all the time in the world. He knew that, as tired as he was, if he rushed, he would almost certainly mess it up. Then when Saenz returned and she worked out what Brighton had been doing, he'd have the devil to pay.

When the work of bending the pen's clip into a crude lock-pick shim was done, Brighton paused for a second to calm down and steady his hands.

Now came the moment of truth. Gritting his teeth and breathing steadily, he worked his shim into the handcuff's lock. Patiently, slowly, he twisted the pen and applied pressure on the lock mechanism inside. Millimetre by millimetre, he twisted, twisted, and twisted . . .

CLICK!

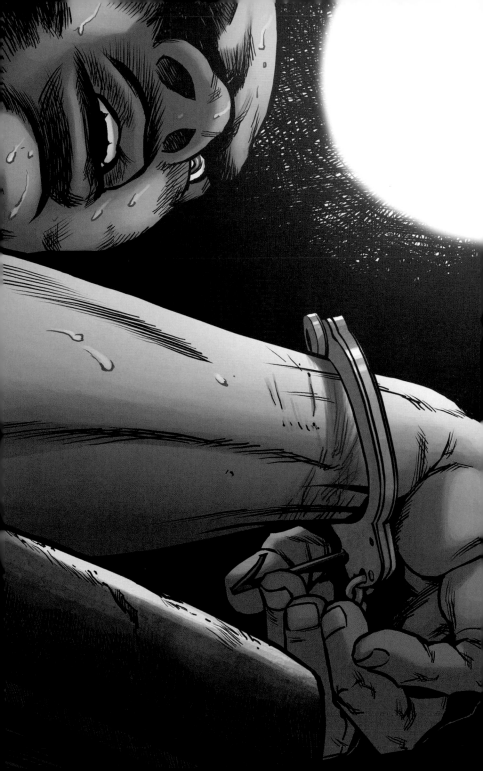

Brighton bit back a howl of triumph as the lock disengaged and the handcuff swung open. Sparing no time to celebrate, he unlocked the cuff from the chair, then began picking the locks on the cuffs around his other hand.

CLICK!

It took all of Brighton's focus to remain calm. He wasn't free yet – both his feet were still bound.

Slowly, calmly, Brighton bent his stiff back and reached down to his feet. He tinkered with the handcuffs on his left foot.

CLICK!

Keeping his focus, he shifted his weight to his other foot. He began to work on the last metal restraints.

CLICK!

Brighton was loose now, but far from free. He gave himself just long enough to let out a deep sigh.

Then he quickly picked and pocketed all four pairs of handcuffs. He slowly stood.

His wrists and ankles alternately itched and burned from where the metal cuffs had chafed him. But those minor pains were nothing compared to the soles of his feet. Saenz had whacked them pretty badly. Escaping on foot with no boots would be rough, especially since he was being held somewhere in the jungle.

But there was nothing he could do about it except tough it out. He couldn't stay there – not if Saenz intended to focus her next session's punishment on his feet as she'd threatened. As much as his feet stung now, he doubted he'd even be able to walk after a day of thrashings.

Gathering his courage, Brighton walked over to the wall beside the door. He could hear two people murmuring in Spanish outside, so he took out two of the sets of handcuffs he'd collected. With steady hands, he doubled one of them up and stuck his fingers through the loops to hold them like a set of brass knuckles.

Brighton bounced the other pair of handcuffs on his palm for a second. Then he tossed them across the room.

KRASSSSSSHH!

The handcuffs struck one of the lights, shattering it. Immediately, the door flew open and two FARC guerillas charged into the room.

The guerillas had almost comical looks of shock on their faces at seeing the chair empty. The sight made Brighton grin.

Taking advantage of their confusion, Brighton leapt out from where he was hiding. He punched the man closest to him in the neck with his makeshift brass knuckles.

THWUNK!

The guerilla staggered, then dropped the M16 he'd been holding. Brighton grabbed it out of the air by the barrel. Then he ducked and spun over to the second man, who was in the process of raising his rifle. Brighton swung the butt of his gun around in a wide arc.

FWUMP!

The butt of the rifle connected with the second guerilla's stomach. A second swing to the head sent the guerilla flat on his back – and out cold. Brighton quickly did the same to the first guerilla.

With both guerillas down for the count, Brighton pulled the camouflage fatigue shirt off one of them. He used the other's belt knife to cut it into two gags.

Brighton cuffed them together, then cuffed them both to the chair. He wrapped the strips of cloth around their mouths to keep the guerillas quiet in case they woke up.

Brighton stuck their knives through his belt, then took the larger man's boots for himself. He pocketed the clip from the first man's M16 and took the other's rifle in his hand.

Armed and confident that the two men weren't going anywhere, Brighton decided it was time to leave. Slowly and carefully, he opened the door and stepped outside.

Emerging from the metal and concrete room, Brighton finally had the chance to get his bearings. It was dark outside, either early morning or late at night, and cooler outside than in the sweatbox he'd been imprisoned in.

Brighton scanned the horizon and saw that the entire area was surrounded by thick jungle. The sound of birds and insects and moving water came from somewhere in the distance.

Not too far away, Brighton heard the sound of power tools being used. He could also hear voices, though not well enough to make out what anyone was saying.

Brighton knew he had two choices. First, he could head directly into the jungle under the cover of darkness and search for running water. Once he found it, he could follow it to either a bigger waterway or straight to civilization – whichever came first. From there, he could find a phone and call in to Shadow Squadron for a pick-up.

That first option was certainly the easiest, safest, and most attractive one. After a day like the one he'd spent with Morgan Saenz, the idea of getting caught again made his skin crawl.

His second option was to finish the mission.

Weary, beaten, and alone, Brighton was at a serious disadvantage. All the same, he decided to finish the job. After all, the Colombians – and Shadow Squadron – were counting on him. The mission was more important than his comfort or even his safety. And being the youngest member on the squad meant he always had something to prove.

And besides, after what FARC had done to him, Brighton liked the idea of throwing a monkey wrench into the works. With any luck, the air strike would shut down their operation. Maybe for good.

With a deep breath, Brighton shut the door behind him. Ahead of him was a narrow, trampled path through the jungle. It led off in the direction where Brighton could hear the sounds of power tools and people talking. He began heading that way himself, though he opted to cut through the jungle and move stealthily.

It turned out to be a good choice. As he reached the far end of the path, he saw that it opened onto a compound crawling with FARC guerillas. In groups of two or three, they patrolled or stood near a sprawling one-story building that straddled a wide, straight stretch of muddy river. From within that building came sounds of construction. Trees stood right up against the sides of the building, their branches providing some camouflage from above. The walls had been painted in a brown and green camo pattern as well. There were no exterior lights visible.

It seemed Brighton had found the hidden FARC shipyard after all. "Lucky me," he muttered.

At least the guerillas had been thoughtful enough to bring him here. Now if only he knew where in the world *here* was . . .

INTEL

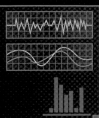

DECRYPTING
IIIII III III III III III III

12345

COM CHATTER

- SINCGARS RADIO - a single-channel ground and airborne radio system used in the field by soldiers
- M4 CARBINE - a short and light selective-fire assault rifle
- MRE - a ready-to-eat, pre-cooked and packaged meal used by soldiers in the US military

3245.98 ● ● ●

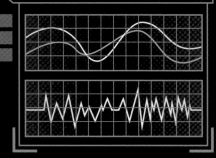

PREY

Brighton skirted the tree line in an arc around the central building. He discovered that the shipyard consisted of four structures other than the one-room shed in which he'd spent the previous hours. They included a main construction facility, a wooden barracks for the soldiers and workers, a barn-sized building full of construction supplies, and a smaller place with an antenna on top and its own generator.

That building has to be the command centre for the guerilla camp, Brighton thought.

The building wasn't much bigger than the tiny base on Malpelo Island where the rest of Shadow

Squadron was holed up. Aside from those buildings, the shipyard also had a row of picnic tables under a tent made of camouflage netting.

There was also a wooden dock downstream from the construction building with speedboats moored there. A guard watched over it. Another guard sat on a stool next to the one-lane, unpaved road leading out into the jungle. Five or ten metres behind that guard, a black off-road motorcycle stood balanced on its kickstand.

Moving slowly in a half-crouch, Brighton made his way to the command centre. He looped through the jungle and came up behind the squat wooden building well out of the guard's line of sight. There were no windows on this side, so all he could do was press his ear to the outside wall and listen. He could hear neither voices nor the sound of people moving around coming from inside. However, he didn't know if that was because no one was inside, or because the walls were just too thick.

In any case, he needed to get inside.

Brighton crept back around the building to the side door that faced the barracks. When he was sure that no one was looking, he darted around the corner and slipped inside.

Brighton closed the door as carefully as he could, but its hinges creaked. Brighton worried that it would give away his position. It was likely that the sound of the generator rumbling on the far side of the building had drowned out the noise, but Brighton froze by the door all the same.

He gripped his stolen rifle tightly just in case the nearest guard came by. Only after two tense minutes of silence did Brighton relax and move on.

Inside, the command centre wasn't much to look at. It was little more than a long corridor with small rooms on either side and a larger meeting room at the far end. The floor was a poured concrete slab, and the walls and doors were made of thin wood. It was humid, stuffy, and it smelled like old sweat. Still, it wasn't bad for a jungle hideout.

Before him were four doors: two on the left, one at the far end of the corridor, and one on the right.

The one at the end was open, showing a dark room with a large table in the middle. All sorts of papers were stuck on the walls.

To Brighton's right was the front of the building, facing toward the centre of the camp. He guessed that the door on that side probably led into a living room. One of the doors on the left was larger than the other. A rim of wan light gleamed around it.

Brighton inched down the corridor. He stopped outside the door to listen. Luckily, there were no lights on in the corridor to throw his shadow underneath the door. He pointed his rifle at the door and leant his ear close to the jamb. The first thing he heard made his blood go cold.

It was Saenz's voice. "It's too hard to predict yet," she was saying in Spanish. "He's definitely American special ops of some kind. His equipment was all state-of-the-art, and he's had some torture-resistance training. He's no coward. Breaking him will take time."

Judging by the silence that followed, Saenz had to be speaking on the phone to someone. Brighton realized he was shaking a little whenever Saenz spoke. Red, crazy thoughts filled his mind at the sound of his torturer's voice calmly discussing how she'd abused him.

For a moment, he considered simply kicking the door open and letting fly with his rifle on full-auto. He'd give Saenz just enough time to recognize him and realize what was about to happen before he pulled the trigger.

But no . . . he couldn't. For one thing, just opening fire would bring every armed guerilla in the camp running. If that happened, Brighton would end up just as dead as Saenz. Add that to the fact that Brighton had never actually shot anybody before. Sure, he'd caused plenty of very bad guys to die, but only indirectly, say by calling in fire support from the air. Even when he'd joined his Shadow Squadron teammates on direct-action missions, he'd never actually engaged in the firefights.

But most importantly, Brighton didn't want his first confirmed kill to involve shooting an unarmed person in cold blood – no matter what she'd done to him.

So Brighton moved on further down the corridor. The second door on the same side as Saenz's room turned out to be a small cupboard full of office supplies and medical supplies. The door that opened out to the front of the building turned out to lead in to a small infirmary with a single bed. The front door of the building led directly into the infirmary. Brighton continued on to the last room, with the table in the middle and the papers stuck up on the walls.

Inside, Brighton grinned. *Jackpot,* he thought. The papers on the walls all proved to be maps. He didn't have sufficient light to read them – the only light in the room was a soft orange glow from the kill switch on a power strip in the corner – but he could at least tell that they were, indeed, maps. There was also a clock on the wall that read *02:15*, which was helpful.

Brighton's eyes lit up with a surge of pure joy when he spotted a very familiar digital-camouflage rucksack in the corner. It was his gear, or at least some of it. Forgetting the maps for the moment, he knelt beside his pack and opened the flap. Right on top was his lifeline back to Shadow Squadron: his SINCGARS field radio.

A few other essentials were left in the pack, including some MREs, a first-aid kit, a compass, and a notebook. But the radio was crucial. It almost made up for the loss of his night-vision goggles, his M4 carbine, all his ammunition, his M84 flashbang grenade, and his smoke grenade.

At least he hadn't brought his AA-12 combat shotgun with him on this mission. He would have been really depressed if he'd lost his baby.

After a quick inventory, he took a back-up torch out of the pack, then stuffed everything else back in. He slipped it on and switched on the torch. With the narrow beam of light, he could read a map without much risk of the enemy spotting him from a distance.

Brighton turned the torch on for a second to scan a few of the maps on the walls. After a moment, he selected two to take with him. The first was a fairly new contour map of this part of the jungle, with the location of the guerilla shipyard conveniently

marked. It also showed overland routes for bringing in supplies and river routes for sneaking narco-subs downstream to the ocean.

The second map was a sea chart. It showed the shipping routes off the Colombian coast that the narco-sub pilots took to Mexico. Brighton pulled out the tacks. He folded the chart as quietly as he could, then stuffed it into a cargo pocket. He studied the contour map a few moments longer before pocketing it along with the torch.

Finally, he raised his M16 and made his way back down the corridor towards the door through which he'd entered the building.

Thus far he'd been lucky to avoid detection. But as he approached the door where he'd heard Morgan Saenz talking, it suddenly opened.

Saenz backed out right into Brighton's path.

Saenz held a torch in one hand and a book tucked under one arm. When she pulled the door shut, she turned and looked right into Brighton's eyes.

Fear and anger flashed in her dark eyes. She opened her mouth to shout. Brighton snapped his rifle up to point at Saenz's neck and shook his head. Saenz immediately closed her mouth.

Brighton jerked his head to the side, motioning for Saenz to go back into the room. Saenz did as she was told, and Brighton followed her into what turned out to be her living quarters. The room had a footlocker, a desk with a laptop computer, and a single bed under a mosquito-net canopy. There was a stack of books in the corner next to the desk. A pair of citronella candles provided dim light.

Saenz turned to face Brighton. "You'll never escape . . ." she said.

"Sit down," Brighton said flatly, nodding at the bed. She did so, never taking her eyes off his.

Brighton took out one of the remaining pairs of handcuffs and tossed it onto the bed next to Saenz. "Cuff your ankle to the bedframe," Brighton ordered her.

Saenz narrowed her eyes but did as he said. "I only have to yell, young man," she said, "and every

FARC soldier in this camp will come to my aid. You might kill me for it, but you won't live long enough to enjoy it."

Brighton smiled at her, his eyes hard as he glared at her over the M16's iron sights. "Go ahead, sister," he challenged. "Yell your head off."

Saenz glared back at him. Then she lowered her eyes. "So now what?" she asked.

"I'm leaving," Brighton said. "I ought to take you prisoner, but that sounds like more trouble than you're worth. You'll probably just jump off the boat the second I take my eyes off you. So you get to stay here, but don't you dare think I'll ever forget about you, Señora Saenz."

Brighton backed out into the corridor and paused. His rifle never wavered, but his mind wasn't so steady. He so badly wanted to pull the trigger and erase Saenz from the world. Who knew how many others would suffer at her hands. And he knew she was just going to raise the alarm and bring everybody running the second he was out of her sight. He might as well get the satisfaction of killing her now while he had the chance . . .

While it might satisfy him to destroy the one who'd hurt him and who knows how many others, Brighton just couldn't bring himself to do it. He had to rise above those impulses if he wanted to be able to look at himself in the mirror tomorrow. He had to be better than the enemy if he wanted to be able to call himself one of the good guys. There was nothing else he could do.

Without another word, he turned and bolted for the side door. He hit it and darted around the corner of the building, desperately hoping that no one happened to be looking his way. It took only that long for Saenz to gather her courage and yell.

"The American has escaped!" she shouted in Spanish. "He's going for the boats! Cut him off!"

Hearing Saenz's shout made Brighton smile. *Sucker,* he thought.

Brighton continued to move along the rear of the building towards the motorcycle on the other side. Saenz kept shouting inside, and the guard who'd been posted on the stool by the one-lane jungle road, presumably Javier, ran back to the dock. He shouted for everyone else to be on the lookout. All the guerillas in earshot sprang into action and fanned out to search. But they were looking in the wrong direction.

Brighton got to the bike to find the keys in the ignition, as he expected. He slung his rifle over one shoulder, hopped on the bike, and kicked it to life. The sound of the engine drew the guerillas' attention like a magnet – and silenced Saenz's yelling for a second. But no one was close enough to do anything to stop him.

He tore off down the supply road. Some of the guards came running and fired a few shots after him, but the bullets pinged harmlessly off the nearby trees.

VROOOOOOOOOOOOOOM!

No one could stop him now.

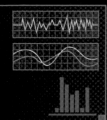

INTEL

DECRYPTING
||||| ||| ||| ||| ||| |||| |||| |||| |

12345

COM CHATTER

- AIRLIFT - a system for transporting people or cargo by aircraft, especially in an emergency

- CALL SIGN - a secret nickname used by the military in radio communications to preserve anonymity to any outside listeners

- OSPREY - an American military tilt-rotor aircraft, capable of vertical and short take-offs and landings

3245.98 ● ● ●

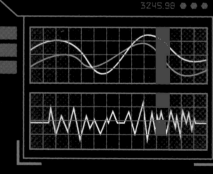

FLIGHT

Morning sunlight illuminated the jungle's canopy. Brighton had long since ditched his stolen motorcycle. Now, he set off overland with his map to find high ground and take the lay of the terrain.

Lying on his belly on a ridge with the guerillas' map beside him, he glanced down at the river that passed through the middle of the FARC camp. He couldn't see the camouflaged shipyard from here, but he knew the geography and landmarks well enough to know exactly where it lay. He set his field radio to the Shadow Squadron's emergency frequency and keyed the transmitter.

"Aerie, this is Eagle," Brighton said, using their call signs. "Aerie, this is Eagle. Do you read me?"

"Eagle!" Lieutenant Commander Ryan Cross answered at once. His voice was full of surprise, delight, and relief. "Eagle, this is Aerie. Give me a status report. Are you all right?"

"I've been better, Commander," Brighton said. "And I'm going to need an airlift here pretty soon."

"The Osprey's already in the air, Eagle," Cross said. "We've been looking for you."

"Good to hear it, Aerie," Brighton said. "But if it's all the same, I need to connect to Major Gaitan first. Little matter of an air strike I promised him."

"Fair enough, Eagle," Cross replied, clearly impressed. "Make your call. We'll be here."

"Roger that," Brighton said. "See you soon, sir. Eagle out."

"Good work out there, Eagle," Cross said. "I knew we could count on you. Aerie out."

Brighton pocketed his radio. "You have no idea, man," he said softly. "No idea."

MISSION DEBRIEFING

OPERATION

EAGLE DOWN

1234

PRIMARY OBJECTIVE

- Covert insertion via parachute

- Rendezvouz with Colombian task force

- Locate shipyard

- Call in co-ordinates for precision air

SECONDARY OBJECTIVES

- Minimize casualties

x Foster positive relations with
  Colombian task force

x Remain undetected

STATUS

5/7 COMPLETE

BRIGHTON, EDGAR

RANK: Staff Sergeant
BRANCH: Air Force Combat
Controller
PSYCH PROFILE: The team's
technician and close-quarters-
combat specialist is popular with
his squadmates but often irritates
his commanding officers.

I've been putting off writing this debriefing, mostly because I'm still mentally sorting out everything that happened to me during *Operation: Nexus*. Between the waterboarding, the stun-gunning, and my interrogator's lousy sense of humour, I was pushed to my breaking point — and beyond. But I trusted in my training, which is the only reason I'm still alive . . . well, that and the ballpoint pen. As for Morgan Saenz, she was picked up a few days ago by the Colombian task force. One guess as to who tipped them off she'd be heading back to Mexico.

— Staff Sergeant Edgar Brighton

2019.591

CREATOR BIO(S)

AUTHOR

CARL BOWEN

Carl Bowen is a father, husband, and writer living in Georgia, USA. He was born in the state of Louisiana, lived briefly in England, and was raised in Georgia, where he went to school. He has published novels, short stories, and comics, and has retold the classic tales 20,000 Leagues Under the Sea, The Strange Case of Dr Jekyll and Mr Hyde, The Jungle Book, Aladdin and the Magic Lamp, Julius Caesar, and The Murders in the Rue Morgue. He is the original author of BMX Breakthrough as well as the Shadow Squadron series.

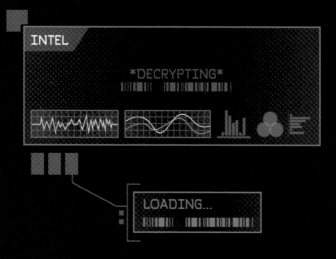

INTEL

DECRYPTING

LOADING...

ARTIST

WILSON TORTOSA

Wilson "Wunan" Tortosa is a Filipino comic book artist best known for his works on *Tomb Raider* and the American relaunch of *Battle of The Planets* for Top Cow Productions. Wilson attended Philippine Cultural High School, then went on to the University of Santo Tomas where he graduated with a Bachelor's Degree in Fine Arts, majoring in Advertising.

COLOURIST

BENNY FUENTES

Benny Fuentes lives in Villahermosa, Tabasco in Mexico, where the temperature is just as hot as the sauce. He studied graphic design in college, but now he works as a full-time colourist in the comic book and graphic novel industry for companies such as Marvel, DC Comics, and Top Cow Productions. He shares his home with two crazy cats, Chelo and Kitty, who act like they own the place.

2019.681

AUTHOR DEBRIEFING

CARL BOWEN

Q/When and why did you decide to become a writer?

A/I've enjoyed writing ever since I was in school. I wrote as much as I could, hoping to become the next Lloyd Alexander or Stephen King, but I didn't sell my first story until I was in college. It had been a long wait, but the day I saw my story in print was one of the best days of my life.

Q/What made you decide to write Shadow Squadron?

A/As a kid, my heroes were always brave knights or noble loners who fought because it was their duty, not for fame or glory. I think the special ops soldiers of the US military embody those ideals. Their jobs are difficult and often thankless, so I wanted to show how cool their jobs are, but also express my gratitude for our brave warriors.

Q/What inspires you to write?

A/My biggest inspiration is my family. My wife's love and support lifts me up when this job seems too hard to keep going. My son is another big inspiration.

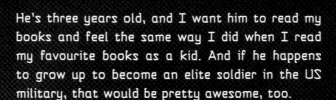

He's three years old, and I want him to read my books and feel the same way I did when I read my favourite books as a kid. And if he happens to grow up to become an elite soldier in the US military, that would be pretty awesome, too.

Q/Describe what it was like to write these books.
A/The only military experience I have is a year I spent in the Army ROTC. It gave me a great respect for the military and its soldiers, but I quickly realized I would have made a pretty awful soldier. I recently got to test out a friend's arsenal of firearms, including a combat shotgun, an AR-15 rifle, and a Barrett M82 sniper rifle. We got to blow apart an old fax machine.

Q/What is your favourite book, movie, and game?
A/My favourite book of all time is *Don Quixote*. It's crazy and it makes me laugh. My favourite movie is either *Casablanca* or *Double Indemnity*, old black-and-white movies made before I was born. My favourite game, hands down, is *Skyrim*, in which you play a heroic dragonslayer. But not even *Skyrim* can keep me from writing more Shadow Squadron stories, so you won't have to wait long to read more about Ryan Cross and his team. That's a promise.

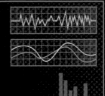
INTEL

```
*DECRYPTING*
```

1234

COM CHATTER

-MISSION PREVIEW: SNIPER SHIELD
Heshem Shadid, an ex-terrorist turned
politician, has requested the US
military's help. Shadid's former friends
are enraged that he has switched sides
and will do anything to take him out.
The intel that Shadid has provided thus
far has proven invaluable to the war
effort in Iraq. He must be protected.

3245.98 ● ● ●

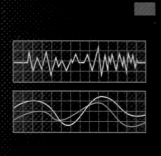

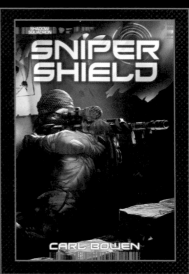

SNIPER SHIELD

Shadow Squadron's unmarked Seahawk helicopter roared in low over the skyline. It paused over the abandoned apartment building. Almost immediately, six members of Shadow Squadron fast-roped down onto the roof. The chopper then hopped over to another building across the street. There, two more team members dropped in, including Kimiyo Yamashita, the team's sniper. These two would act as overwatch for the rest of the team, picking off any insurgents who tried to escape.

So far, the operation was proceeding smoothly. Cross and his second-in-command, Chief Petty Officer Alonso Walker, led the six-man squad down into the building. They made their way through the structure slowly, checking blind spots and covering each other's backs. They encountered no resistance –

until they reached the ground floor. Cross and his men had caught the insurgents in the middle of lunch. To say they were caught unprepared would be an understatement.

Cross squeezed the trigger of his M4 carbine.

BANG!

BANG! Cross fired a single round into the ceiling as a warning shot. One of the Iraqis sprinted out of the room. The rest of the insurgents fell over themselves trying to surrender.

Cross motioned for Walker and Sergeant Mark Shepherd to join him in pursuit of the fleeing hostile. The remaining three members of Shadow Squadron stayed behind to secure the non-combatants.

Cross chased the fleeing insurgent down a corridor and around a corner. Suddenly, the insurgent popped out from a half-open door with an AK-47 in his hand.

RAT-TAT-TAT-TAT-TAT!

The Iraqi sprayed bullets wildly at Cross and his men. Ducking out of harm's way just in time, Cross reached around the corner with his rifle to throw out

suppressing fire. The spray forced the Iraqi back into his hole, and also bought enough time for Walker and Shepherd to rush around the corner and get into their respective cover positions down the corridor.

When the insurgent stuck his head out to see once again, he was surprised to see all three Americans open fire. Chief Walker managed to hit the Iraqi in the side by firing straight through the cheap drywall beside the door frame. At the same time, a one-in-a-million shot from Cross popped the insurgent in the wrist.

The man's rifle skittered away down the corridor.

The injured man retreated back into the room. Before Chief Walker could close in on him, the Iraqi kicked the door shut. Then he locked it.

Cross, Walker, and Shepherd huddled together just outside the locked door. Walker and Shepherd glanced at Cross for orders. Cross took a position to the left of the door and motioned Walker to the opposite side. He signalled for Shepherd to get ready to kick the door in.

Cross tapped the small button on the two-way

canal phone tucked into his right ear. "Fire Team Two, report," Cross said, whispering just loud enough for the tiny earbud radio to pick up his voice.

"All clear here, sir," Staff Sergeant Adam Paxton replied on the line. "The only man not accounted for is the one you went after."

"Good, we'll bring him round," Cross answered quietly. "Out." He paused for a moment to let the line clear, then tapped his canal phone again. "Overwatch, report."

"No rats, sir," Staff Sergeant Edgar Brighton reported. The USAF Combat Controller was stationed on the roof across the street with Lieutenant Kimiyo Yamashita, the team's sniper. While Yamashita scanned the building and the street through the Leupold scope of his M110 sniper rifle, Brighton scanned the area through the high-resolution camera on his remote-controlled reconnaissance UAV quad-copter. "No sign of reinforcements, either."

"Good," Cross replied. "Out."

' Yamashita said. "Your fugitive is holed
ᴐm on the south face of the building,
‗ght?"

Cross took a moment to check his relative
position in the building. "Affirmative," Cross said.
"Do you have a visual on our target?"

"I can tell which room he went into, but I don't
have a shot from this vantage point," Yamashita
said. "I'm relocating now."

"Roger that," Cross said. "Out."

"Sir," Chief Walker said when comm-traffic in
the team's canal phones stopped. He nodded at
the closed door between them and the wounded
Al-Qaeda insurgent. "Let me try to talk to him. I can
get him to come out."

Shepherd looked sceptical, but didn't say
anything. Cross had his doubts, too.

"He can't be more than eighteen years old, sir,"
Walker said, reading their expressions. "He's been
shot twice already and he's probably scared to
death. Let me give him a chance to surrender. He'll
take it."

Cross knew all about the chief's optimistic faith in humanity and how it occasionally clouded his judgement. However, Cross didn't like the idea of kicking in the door and gunning down a scared teenager any more than Walker did. So, with a nod, Cross motioned at the door. He kept his M4 ready, though, as did Shepherd.

"Son, I want you to listen to me," Walker spoke in Arabic, leaning against the door. "I know you're in pain, and I know you're losing blood. I know you're scared. But if you work with me, I can get you out of this mess without –"

"I have a way out!" the insurgent barked back. "You'll see!"

The desperation in the boy's voice made Cross nervous, but at least it gave him a good sense of where the insurgent was standing. Cross exchanged a look with Shepherd, making sure the Green Beret would be ready to breach the door. Shepherd nodded.

"Let's talk about this," Walker said, his voice calm and steady, as if he were talking to one of his own kids back home. "What's your name?"

"Don't pretend you care who I am," the insurgent snarled in Arabic. "All you care about is –"

The boy's words stopped short as a muffled thump sounded from within the room. Cross thought he'd heard a sound like glass breaking. After a moment, everything was silent. Cross didn't like that.

Cross signalled for Shepherd to breach the door. Ignoring the frustration on Walker's face, Shepherd launched himself across the corridor.

CRUNCH!

Shepherd bashed the door off its hinges with a powerful kick. Cross and Walker were right on his heels, then the three of them spread out to cover the room in all directions.

No sooner were they through the door when Yamashita's voice came over their canal phones. "Clear," the sniper said.

"Clear," Cross confirmed. As he glanced around the room, he saw that a nearby table was piled with explosives – and the fallen insurgent held the detonator in his hand . . .

TRANSMISSION ERROR

PLEASE CONTACT YOUR LOCAL LIBRARY
OR BOOKSHOP FOR MORE INFORMATION...

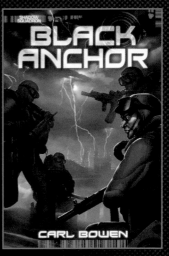

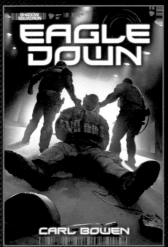

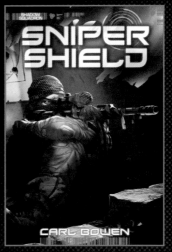

www.raintreepublishers.co.uk

SAVING...

LOGGING OUT...

2012.101